The Boy Who Drew Cats

ADAPTED BY
MARGARET HODGES

ILLUSTRATED BY
AKI SOGABE

Holiday House / New York

Adapted from Lafcadio Hearn's *Japanese Fairy Tales*,
Boni and Liveright: New York, 1918.
Adaptation copyright © 2002 by Margaret Hodges
Illustrations copyright © 2002 by Aki Sogabe
All Rights Reserved
Printed in the United States of America
www.holidayhouse.com
First Edition

The text typeface is Hiroshige.
The artwork was created with cut paper, watercolor,
and airbrush.

Library of Congress Cataloging-in-Publication Data
Hodges, Margaret, 1911–
The boy who drew cats / adapted by Margaret Hodges;
pictures by Aki Sogabe.—1st ed.
p. cm.
Adapted from Lafcadio Hearn's Japanese Fairy Tales,
Boni and Liveright: New York 1918.
Summary: A young boy's obsession
with drawing cats changes his life.
ISBN 0-8234-1594-5 (hardcover)
[1. Fairy tales. 2. Folklore—Japan. 3. Cats—Folklore.
4. Artists—Folklore.]
I. Sogabe, Aki, ill. II. Hearn, Lafcadio,
1850–1904. III. Title.

PZ8.H653 Bo 2002
398.2'0952'02—dc21
[E]   2001016642

To Old Kitty
with whom we lived so long
M. H.

To Ryan
and Sandy
A. S.

In a small country village in Japan, there once lived a poor farmer and his wife, who were very good people. They had several children and found it hard to feed them all. The oldest son, when only fourteen years old, was strong enough to help his father, and the little girls learned to help their mother almost as soon as they could walk.

But the youngest child, a little boy, did not seem to be fit for hard work. He was very clever, more clever than all his brothers and sisters, but he was quite weak and small, and people said he would never grow very big. So his parents thought it would be better for him to become a priest rather than a farmer.

They took him to the village temple one day and asked the good
old priest who lived there if he would teach their little boy all that a
priest ought to know. The old man spoke kindly to the lad, and
asked him some hard questions. So clever were the answers, the
priest agreed to take the little fellow into the temple and to educate
him for the priesthood.

The boy learned quickly what the old priest taught him and was very obedient in most things. But he had one fault. He liked to draw cats during study hours and to draw cats even where cats ought not to have been drawn at all.

Whenever he found himself alone, he drew cats. He drew them on the margins of the priest's books, and on all the screens of the temple, and on the walls, and on the pillars. Several times the priest told him this was not right, but the boy did not stop drawing cats. He drew them because he really could not help it.

 One day when he had drawn some very clever pictures of cats on a paper screen, the old priest said to him severely, "My boy, you must go away from this temple at once. You will never make a good priest, but perhaps you will become a great artist. Now let me give you a last piece of advice, and be sure you never forget it. *Avoid large places at night; keep to small.*"

The boy did not know what the priest meant by saying, *"Avoid large places; keep to small."* He thought and thought while he was tying up his little bundle of clothes to go away, but he could not understand those words, and he was afraid to speak to the priest anymore, except to say good-bye.

He left the temple very sorrowfully, and began to wonder what he should do. He felt sure his father would punish him for having been disobedient to the priest, so he was afraid to go home.

All at once he remembered that at the next village, twelve miles away, there was a very big temple. He had heard there were several priests at that temple, and he made up his mind to go to them.

Now the boy did not know it, but that big temple was closed up.
A goblin had frightened the priests away and had taken possession
of the place. Some brave warriors had afterward gone to the temple
at night to kill the goblin, but they had never been seen alive again.
Nobody had ever told these things to the boy, so he walked all the
way to the village, hoping to be treated kindly by the priests.

When he got to the village, it was already dark and all the people were in bed. But he saw the big temple on a hill at the other end of the widest street, and he saw there was a light in the temple. People who tell the story say the goblin used to make that light in order to tempt lonely travelers to ask for shelter.

The boy went at once to the temple and knocked. There was no sound inside. He knocked and knocked again, but still nobody came. At last he pushed gently at the door and was quite glad to find it had not been fastened. So he went in. He saw a lamp burning but no priest.

行無常

He thought some priest would be sure to come very soon, and he sat down and waited. Then he noticed that everything in the temple was gray with dust and thickly spun over with cobwebs. So he thought to himself that the priests would certainly like to have the place cleaned. He wondered why they had allowed everything to get so dusty. What pleased him, however, were some big white screens, good to paint cats upon. Though he was tired, he looked at once for a paintbrush and ink. He found them, and began to paint cats.

He painted a great many cats upon the screens. Then he felt very, very sleepy. He was just on the point of lying down to sleep beside one of the screens when he suddenly remembered the words *"Avoid large places at night; keep to small."*

The temple was very large. He was all alone, and as he thought of these words—though he did not quite understand them—he began for the first time to feel a little afraid. He resolved to look for a small place in which to sleep. He found a little cabinet with a sliding door, went into it, and shut the door. Then he lay down and fell fast asleep.

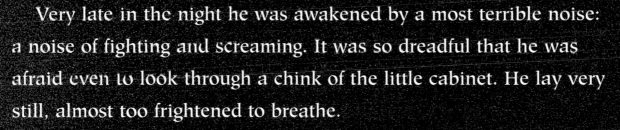

Very late in the night he was awakened by a most terrible noise: a noise of fighting and screaming. It was so dreadful that he was afraid even to look through a chink of the little cabinet. He lay very still, almost too frightened to breathe.

The light that had been in the temple went out, but the awful sounds continued, and became more awful, and all the temple shook. After a long time, silence came, but the boy was still afraid to move. He did not move until the light of the morning sun shone into the cabinet through the chinks of the little door.

Then he got out of his hiding place very cautiously and looked about. The first thing he saw was that all the floor of the temple was covered with blood. And then he saw, lying dead in the middle of it, an enormous, monstrous rat—a goblin bigger than a cow!

But who or what could have killed it? There was no man or
other creature to be seen. Suddenly the boy observed that the
mouths of all the cats he had drawn the night before were red and
wet with blood. Then he knew that the goblin had been killed by
the cats he had drawn. And then, for the first time, he understood
why the wise old priest had said to him, "Avoid large places at
night; keep to small."

Afterward, that boy became a very famous artist. Some of the cats that he drew are still shown to travelers in Japan. And parents show the drawings to their children. "This is the work of Sesshu Toyo," they say. "Now everyone knows his name, but once he was just a boy who drew cats, just a child like you."

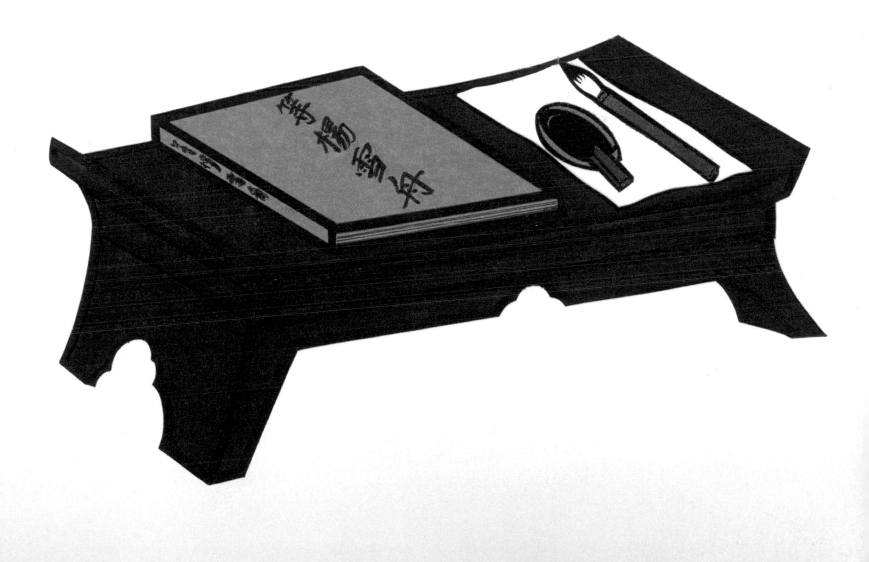

ABOUT THIS STORY

The Boy Who Drew Cats is based on a legend about the celebrated fifteenth-century Japanese artist Sesshu Toyo, whose ink drawings at a Zen monastery were said to be so realistic that they would sometimes spring to life. Lafcadio Hearn was the son of a Greek mother and an Irish father, but he fell in love with the culture of Ancient Japan. Writing and teaching in Japan, he won fame with his retellings of tales and legends learned from his Japanese wife, their children, his students, and other Japanese friends.

This story was originally published
as a pamphlet in Tokyo
by Takejiro Hasegawa.
I adapted it
from Lafcadio Hearn's
Japanese Fairy Tales,
Boni and Liveright:
New York, 1918.